MILLY'S WEDDING

KATE SUMMERS

Illustrated by MAGGIE KNEEN

Dutton Children's Books

NEW YORK

Text copyright © 1998 by Kate Summers

Illustrations copyright © 1998 by Maggie Kneen

All rights reserved.

CIP Data is available.

Published in the United States 1999 by Dutton Children's Books,

a division of Penguin Putnam Books for Young Readers

375 Hudson Street, New York, New York 10014

Originally published in Great Britain 1998 by Orion Children's Books, London

Typography by Alan Carr

Printed in Italy

First American Edition

ISBN 0-525-46046-2

2 4 6 8 10 9 7 5 3 1

Milly Town Mouse was getting married.
One moonlit night, she had met Tom Brown
Mouse down by the canal.

Tom was on a bank, nibbling cheese.
Milly was by the bridge.
They looked. They blinked.

And fell in love.

In the days that followed, Tom and Milly often
went walking along the towpath. Milly loved
the brightly painted boats docked up and down
the canal.

One day Tom showed Milly where he lived.
He took her to a houseboat, beautifully
decorated, with flowers growing on the deck.

"Come aboard," said Tom.

The boat was rocking gently. Milly could hear the water lap-lap-lapping against the side. "I wish it would keep still!" she said.

So Tom took Milly by the paw and helped her onto the boat.

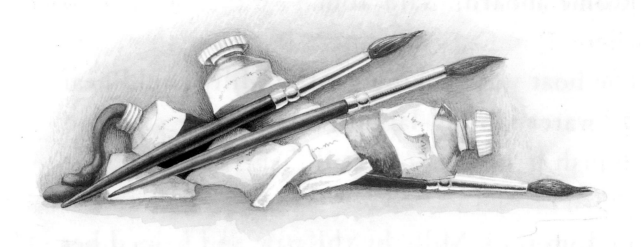

Milly followed Tom down a ladder, to a room below the deck. It was full of pictures, paper, and paint, all jumbled together.
"Goodness!" said Milly with a sigh.

Tom pointed to a portrait on the wall.
"That's me," he said.

"You have very fine whiskers," said Milly.

Then the two mice climbed up inside a cupboard, where Tom had made himself a home.

"I know it's not much of a place *now*," he said, "but with some wallpaper, tables, chairs . . . ANYTHING you like. I could make the best house for . . . us. Oh, Milly! Will you marry me?"

"Yes," said Milly. "I will!"

And so Tom and Milly were
engaged to be married.
Tom gave Milly a heart-shaped
corsage of lavender to wear.

Milly took Tom to meet her parents.
Mr. and Mrs. Town Mouse thought Tom would
make a very good husband for their daughter.

Then they all got busy with plans for the ceremony. There was so much to do and not very much time before the wedding day.

Tom and Milly sent invitations to their relatives and friends. Lots of invitations! They had brothers and sisters all over town.

And of course
Milly wanted her best friend,
Tilly Country Mouse,
to come to the wedding.
"I must go and see her at once," Milly told Tom.
"I have something important to ask her."

Early the next morning, Milly set off for the country. It was a long walk, but at last she found the little lane that led to Tilly's house.

Tilly was very excited to see her friend again. She squeaked with happiness when she heard Milly's news. "Will you be my maid of honor?" asked Milly. "Of course!" said Tilly. "I'll make your wedding dress, too."

After a lunch of freshly baked
bread and hazelnut butter, they
looked at dress patterns together.
They chose ones that were just
right for Milly and her bridesmaids.

"How many bridesmaids will there be?" asked Tilly.
"Six," said Milly. "There's Berry, Pip, Clover, Lily,
and the twins, Hope and April."

Tilly took Milly's measurements carefully. Then
she cut out the pattern in paper and pinned the
pieces together. "Tomorrow," she said, "we shall
buy the very best silk for your dress."

The next day, Tilly took Milly to a big mulberry tree. It was full of silkworms eating leaves.

Tilly told Milly that they were making silk. "Each silkworm spins a cocoon from fine sticky threads," she explained. "Each tiny thread becomes a strand of glossy silk."

At the foot of the tree they found Mrs. Weaver Mouse. She was winding the silk strands onto spools, ready for the loom.

And piled high were bolts of silk in the prettiest colors— apple blossom, peach, apricot, fern green— every color you could imagine.

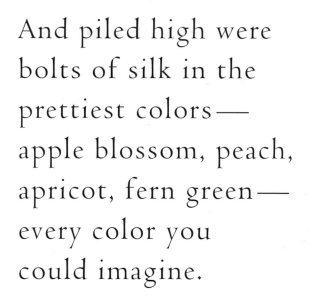

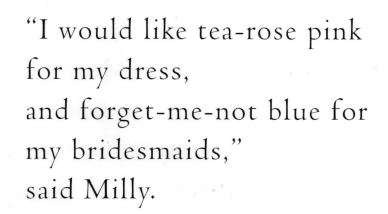

"I would like tea-rose pink for my dress, and forget-me-not blue for my bridesmaids," said Milly.

While Milly was in the country, Tom was busy on the boat. He was a handy mouse, clever with his paws at carpentry and plumbing.

Some of Tom's friends came to help, too. Together they planned to turn the cupboard into a splendid home in no time!

They found everything they needed lying on the floor of the houseboat. Soon there was the sound of many mice

hammering,

sawing,

scrubbing,

plastering,

scraping,

and wallpapering,   all at once.

One afternoon, Tom decided to fix up the bathroom. When he turned on the water, the shower spun around and around.

Before he could turn off the taps, he was in a puddle right up to his knees.

At that moment, Tom's uncle, a seafaring mouse called Captain Longtail, arrived. "Ahoy there, Tom!" he said. "You look as wet as a fish!"

While Tom was mopping
up the mess, he told his
uncle all about Milly.

When Milly arrived back
from the country,
Tom introduced them to each other.

"I'll perform the ceremony myself," said Captain
Longtail. "I've married lots of couples at sea,
but yours will be the grandest wedding of
the year!"

At last it was Milly's wedding day. Tilly arrived early at Milly's house. She was followed by the excited little bridesmaids, each carrying a box with her dress neatly packed inside.

Tilly opened the biggest box and showed Milly her bridal gown. Milly gasped. "It's *beautiful*," she said. "Oh, Tilly! You are the most clever mouse in the world!"

Tilly laughed. "Let me help you put it on," she said. "I only hope it fits."

Milly's dress was like a summer rose in full bloom.
Tilly had embroidered the bodice with hearts and
flowers and had stitched a tiny silver acorn,
for luck.

Milly twirled around
and around in front
of the mirror.
She looked lovely,
and the dress
fit perfectly.

"Can I put my dress on now?"
asked Lucy, the youngest
bridesmaid.

"Of course," said Tilly.
"It's time for all of us to get ready."

Back at the boat, Tom was
putting on his tuxedo. His
brother Sam, who had agreed to
be Tom's best mouse, was there, too.

"Have you got the ring?" Tom asked anxiously.
"Yes," said Sam.
"Where?" said Tom.
"In my pocket," said Sam.
"Which one?" said Tom.
"This one," said Sam,
patting his vest.
"Don't worry. It's very safe with me."

Then Tom tried on his top hat.
But, oh dear! It was much too big.
"The shop has sent the wrong
size!" cried Tom.

Sam looked at his watch. There wasn't much time.
The wedding would start in less than an hour!
He would have to hurry.

So he ran as fast as he could to the shop to buy
a smaller hat. On the way back, he took a shortcut
across the canal, skipping from barge to barge.

He took a flying leap onto the towpath,

tripped over a coil of rope and . . .

SPLASH! The ring fell
out of his pocket and into the water!

Sam could see the ring glinting in the sun, and it was sinking fast. He thought quickly. If he used Tom's hat for a boat, perhaps he could fish it out.

Sam launched the hat by pushing off the bank with a twig. He had to hurry!

Sam leaned over the brim as far as he dared, hooked the ring with his twig, and grasped it with his paw.

"Phew!" he sighed. "That was close."

Back at the houseboat, Tom was pacing up and down, looking worried.

"There you are!" he said to Sam. "That took a long time!"

"I'm sorry," said Sam. "I stopped to . . . er . . . do a little fishing."

"So I see," said Tom. "My hat is dripping wet! Oh, well. We'd better get ready to go. You've still got the ring, right?"

Up on deck, Captain Longtail had ordered his crew to form an honor guard. The mouse sailors looked very handsome in their uniforms as they stood at attention.

As the first guests arrived, the musicians began to play a tune.

Soon the deck was crowded with happy, chattering mice, all wearing their best coats and gowns.

The mother of the bride arrived, dressed in green, with satin shoes to match. Milly's grandmother wore velvet and a bonnet trimmed with lace.

You never saw so many good-looking mice together all at once!

At exactly twelve o'clock,
the bridal party arrived.

Milly and her father sat in a carriage pulled by
two shiny stag beetles. Tilly and the young
bridesmaids came in a wagon.

Mr. Town Mouse helped his daughter down from the carriage. When everyone was ready, they walked up the gangplank onto the houseboat.

Tom was waiting for Milly on deck. He thought she was the most beautiful mouse he had ever seen. Milly smiled as she took his paw.

The wedding had begun.

Captain Longtail read the marriage vows from a book while Tom and Milly listened carefully. They promised to love and care for each other always.

Then Sam passed the ring to Tom, and Tom and Milly exchanged rings. "You may kiss the bride," said the captain.

And so Tom and Milly were married.

Afterward Mr. and Mrs. Brown Mouse had the photographer take some pictures. It took quite a long time.

First there were pictures of the bride and groom, Milly and Tom.

Then there were pictures of the bridesmaids . . .

and Tom with Sam . . . and Milly with Tilly . . .

and, last of all, Tom and Milly with . . .

EVERYONE!

"Now let's eat!" said Tom. "I'm hungry!"
He and Milly led the way to an enormous table
spread with a wonderful wedding feast.

When everyone had eaten and drunk as much as
they were able, Sam stood up and gave a toast to
the bride and groom. Then he tried to tell them
all about the ring and how he had used Tom's
hat as a boat.
Everybody laughed until
the tears rolled down
their cheeks. But
nobody believed him—
except Tom.

Then Tom and Milly cut their wedding cake.

It was made of tier upon
tier of the richest,
creamiest
cheesecake
imaginable.
Each slice
was a
mouth-
watering
delight.

Later that evening,
when Milly and Tom were
alone, Milly whispered,
"I love you,
Tom Brown Mouse."
"I love you, too,"
said Tom.

And they danced in the glow
of the pale harvest moon.